• I AM READING •

GRANDAD'S DINOSAUR

BROUGH GIRLING

Illustrated by
STEPHEN DELL

Kingfisher

KINGFISHER

An imprint of Larousse plc
New Penderel House, 283-288 High Holborn
London WC1V 7HZ

First published by Kingfisher 1997
2 4 6 8 10 9 7 5 3

Educational Adviser: Prue Goodwin
Reading and Language Centre
University of Reading

A CIP catalogue record for this book
is available from the British Library.

ISBN 1 85697 483 9

Printed in Singapore

Contents

Chapter One

This is Sally.

And this is

Sally's grandad.

Sally's grandad has a rather untidy garden with a pond.

Grandad said Sally could try to catch some tadpoles in the pond.

So Sally went to the garage to get a fishing-net.

Sally's grandad

has a rather untidy garage.

Sally couldn't find a fishing-net anywhere.

She looked under some boxes . . .

She looked on a shelf . . .

She looked in a cupboard . . .

but there was no fishing-net.

Then Sally heard a rustling noise.

It was coming from behind

a pile of old magazines . . .

Suddenly,

out jumped the strangest creature

Sally had ever seen.

It was bright red

and about the size of a large dog.

Sally was amazed.

"Hello there!" said the creature.

Sally was even more amazed.

"You must be Sally!

I've heard your grandad

talking about you."

Sally looked frightened.

"Don't be scared,"

said the creature.

"I'm only

a dinosaur!"

"A dinosaur!" said Sally.

"Oh, I know people think of dinosaurs as great big creatures with long tails and tall necks," the dinosaur went on.

"And everyone thinks we died out ages ago. But there are a few of us little ones still around. It's just that humans don't often spot us. You have to be very quick, and very lucky, to see a dinosaur."

And he smiled at Sally.

APD 1

"But why didn't Grandad tell me

about you?" asked Sally,

feeling rather cross.

"Because *he* doesn't know about me,"

said the dinosaur.

"He's not quick enough . . .

or lucky enough . . .

to see me."

"Now then,

have you seen the fishing-net?"

asked the dinosaur.

"I was looking for it when you came in."

"To catch tadpoles?" asked Sally.

"Good gracious, no!" he replied.

"I want some pondweed for my dinner.

I used to live in a lovely warm swamp

where there was

plenty of pondweed.

It's my favourite!

Come on, let's get going!"

And he handed Grandad's best fishing-net to Sally.

Chapter Two

Sally and the small red dinosaur

started to walk down the garden path.

Suddenly, the dinosaur spotted

Grandad's washing-line.

It was covered in clothes

that Grandad had washed

that morning.

"Hey!" said the dinosaur.

"Look at that!

I just love those crazy things!"

"What things?" said Sally.

"Those crazy

wishy-washy-whirly-giggy things!

Have you ever had a spin on one?"

"What do you mean?" asked Sally.

"I'll show you!" grinned the dinosaur.

Before Sally knew what was happening,

the dinosaur leapt on to

Grandad's washing-line

and started to spin round and round.

"WHEEEEEE!!!

Watch me go!"

Very soon the washing
started to fly off the line.
A stripey towel went first,
then a pair of swimming trunks,
and one of Grandad's old string vests.
Sally started to laugh.

Then she heard the creak
of a window opening!
In a flash,
the dinosaur dropped
to the ground
and hid behind
a tub of flowers.

“Sally!” called Grandad.

“My whiskers!

The wind has started to blow a bit,

hasn’t it?

Put that washing back on the line,

there’s a good girl.”

And Grandad shut the window

with a bang.

Sally started to pick up the washing.

"Do you think he saw us?"

asked the dinosaur

from behind the flowers.

"I don't think so," said Sally.

Chapter Three

Sally and the small red dinosaur started to walk on down the path.

"Hey! Look at that!" said the dinosaur suddenly.

"There's one of those fab
off-you-go-scooty-carts!
I love them!"
The dinosaur was pointing
to a small handcart.
Sally's grandad used it
to move his dustbin
from the back door
to the garden gate.
"Have you ever
had a ride on one?"
asked the dinosaur.
"Quick! Jump on!"
Before Sally knew what was happening,
the dinosaur was on the cart.

Sally got on behind him.

The dinosaur scooted the cart along with one back leg.

He steered with his front paws.

“WHIZZO!!!” shouted the dinosaur.

They went very fast down the garden path.

“How do we stop?” cried Sally.

“Easy!” said the dinosaur.

The next moment they crashed

SLAP!

BANG!

right into

Grandad's dustbin!

The cart,

Sally,

and the small red dinosaur

flew through the air . . .

and landed in the cabbage patch.

The lid of the dustbin
fell on the garden path
with a mighty clatter.
It sounded like an elephant
walking into a drum kit.

Then Sally heard
the creak of a window opening.

"Sally!" called Grandad.

"My whiskers! Now the wind has

blown off the dustbin lid!

Put it back for me,

there's a good girl."

"Yes, Grandad," said Sally.

"Do you think he saw us?"

whispered the dinosaur.

"I don't think so," said Sally.

Chapter Four

Sally and the small red dinosaur came to the garden hose and sprinkler lying on the lawn.

"Hey! Look at that!" cried the dinosaur.
"A sprinkly-winkly-roundy-wetter!
Great! Turn the water on, Sally,
and watch me go!"

Sally turned it on and waited.

Then the dinosaur did an amazing thing.

As the sprinkler started to go round,

he stood in the middle of it.

Then he began to do all sorts

of clever tricks.

As the sprinkler
went faster,
the dinosaur
balanced on
one leg.

He did a
handstand.

He even stood
on his head.

"WHOOOOOOSH!!!
Speed it up, Sally!
This is fantastic!"

Sally turned the water full on,
and went to join in the fun.
She ran round and round
the spinning dinosaur
until she began to feel
quite dizzy.
The water splashed everywhere
and they both got very wet!

"You're fantastic, too!" giggled Sally.
"I didn't know dinosaurs could be like you!"

The dinosaur went faster

and faster

and faster!

Then he began to wobble.

Just when he was trying

a very difficult tail-stand,

the sprinkler tipped over.

A jet of water

sprayed into Sally's face.

As Sally tried to get out of the way,

her feet got mixed up

with the dinosaur's feet.

They both tripped over the hose,

and each other.

But they didn't fall on the wet lawn . . .

they fell into Grandad's garden pond!

Then they heard

the creak of a window opening.

"Sally!" called Grandad.

"My whiskers!

Now it's started to rain.

You'd better come in,

there's a good girl."

"Yes, Grandad," said Sally,

still sitting in the cold muddy water.

“Do you think he saw us?”

asked the dinosaur.

“I don’t think so,” said Sally,

as she got out of the pond

and dripped back towards the house.

Chapter Five

Later that evening,

Sally and Grandad were reading

a book together.

The book was called

The Wonderful World of Dinosaurs.

There were lots of pictures
of great big dinosaurs
with long tails and tall necks.

Suddenly, Sally spotted
a *small* dinosaur.
It was red.
It looked *exactly* like the dinosaur
in Grandad's garage.
"Hey, look at that!" cried Sally.
"My whiskers!" said Grandad.

"I didn't know
there were any *red* dinosaurs!
This one was called a
DO-YOU-THINK-HE-SAURUS.
The book says sometimes people are still
lucky enough to see one!
But I don't believe that, do you, Sally?"

Sally started to giggle . . .

and so did somebody else!

About the Author and Illustrator

Brough Girling has written a lot of books for children, including the popular *Vera Pratt* series. He lives in Oxfordshire where he and his wife keep some sheep, chickens, ducks and a cow. "But sadly," says Brough, "we don't have any red dinosaurs . . . at least we've never seen one!"

Stephen Dell has been working in advertising for many years, but *Grandad's Dinosaur* is his first book. He says, "I really enjoyed drawing the little dinosaur getting up to so much mischief - I wish I'd met a dinosaur when I was younger!" Stephen lives in London with his wife and baby daughter.

If you've enjoyed reading *Grandad's Dinosaur*,
try these other **I Am Reading** books:

ALLIGATOR TAILS AND CROCODILE CAKES
Nicola Moon & Andy Ellis

BARN PARTY
Claire O'Brien & Tim Archbold

KIT'S CASTLE
Chris Powling & Anthony Lewis

MISS WIRE AND THE THREE KIND MICE
Ian Whybrow & Emma Chichester Clark

MR COOL
Jacqueline Wilson & Stephen Lewis

PRINCESS ROSA'S WINTER
Judy Hindley & Margaret Chamberlain

WATCH OUT, WILLIAM
Kady MacDonald Denton